ROSES FOR GITA

by Rachna Gilmore

Illustrated by Alice Priestley

SECOND STORY Press

Gita tied another small bell on the wire. Done. She shook the wind chimes and the bells tinkled. Gita laughed. They didn't sound like her grandmother Naniji's singing, but they would still make music for the garden. Gita would hang them on the fence right above where the First Rose would be planted. She always thought of it with capital letters — the First Rose, for their new garden for their new home. It had to be a climbing rose, of course — Naniji's favourite.

Right now, the yard was just boring grass, except in the wild overgrown corner where the fence was broken between their yard and mean old Mr. Flinch's. But soon, soon it would be bursting with colour, with twisty paths, surprise corners — just like Naniji's garden in India.

Gita put away the leftover bells in the package Naniji had sent, and ran to the dining room.

"Will we get the First Rose today, Mummy?" Gita looked anxiously at the papers scattered on the table.

Mummy rubbed her face. "I have to finish this, Gita. We'll go tomorrow, okay?"

Ever since Mummy went back to university everything was "tomorrow". Everything but her work.

Gita wandered outside to the deep, wide hole she'd dug for the First Rose. Naniji said roses needed space so the roots could grow strong. But what good was the widest hole without a rose bush?

Gita climbed on the picnic table and cautiously looked over the fence. Good — no sign of Mr. Flinch. She straightened up slowly to get a glimpse of his rose-covered archway. How did that crazy old man have such a lovely garden?

She peered through her eyelashes until the flowers blended into streams of colour. It was early morning in Naniji's garden. She and Naniji were wandering together, snipping dead blooms, cutting fresh flowers, pulling weeds. The sky was purpley-pink, cool, like Naniji's humming. She always hummed in the garden, sometimes high, sometimes low, like the wind. Flowers grew better, she said, if you sang to them. Gita's throat tightened. Could she hear Naniji humming?

She heard a low rumbling. A bee? Gita opened her eyes. Mr. Flinch, mumbling to himself, shuffled around the corner. Before she could move he growled, "Boy, get down off there. Stop bothering me."

Gita jumped down, heart hammering. Mean old man with his ugly squinty eyes. Always calling her boy, snapping at her.

Once Gita had wandered into his garden and he'd shouted, "Boy, how many times do I have to tell you? Out, I say, out."

Gita stuck out her tongue at the fence. You had to be really nasty to mind anyone just *looking* at your garden. Naniji was always showing people around hers, giving away flowers. They grew better, she said, when they were shared. Mr. Flinch's flowers should all be dead.

Gita woke at sunrise the next morning. She could almost hear Naniji strolling through the garden, singing. Gita dressed and ran outside. A cool breeze murmured over the fence. What was that sound? Music?

Gita squirmed through the shrubs in the corner of her yard. She crept towards the rose arbour and peered through the roses. Someone was playing the violin. Soft and sweet, swaying with the music. It was Mr. Flinch — his face gentle, glowing with delight.

The roses blurred into soft splashes. Gita wiped her face against her sleeve and tiptoed away.

In her room, Gita shook the wind chimes. When they stopped singing she put them in a bag with a note:

> *Mr. Flinch,*
> *These are wind chimes I made. You can hang*
> *them in your garden for the roses. My name is*
> *Gita. I'm not a boy. I'm a girl. I moved in next*
> *door three months ago.*

Before she could change her mind, she ran outside and put the bag in Mr. Flinch's mailbox.

Back in her own yard, Gita stared at the empty hole waiting for the First Rose. She swallowed the lump in her throat. Naniji's garden was miles and miles away. She flopped down and buried her face in her knees.

She wasn't sure how long she'd sat there when she heard a soft tinkling. She was imagining things. There were no flowers, no singing, nothing.

"Ahem!"

Gita lifted her head.

Mr. Flinch, holding the wind chimes, peered over the fence. The glasses he wore made his eyes big and blurry. Monster eyes.

Gita's heart thumped.

"Well, now, you're a girl all right." Mr. Flinch's voice was creaky and surprised, not shouting or muttering. "Don't those boys live here anymore?"

Gita shook her head.

"Well! I never knew. Can't see much without my glasses. Those boys were always tearing through my flower beds, and ... I didn't know they'd gone." The monster eyes stared at her. "You, er, Gita, then? Did you give me this?"

"Yes. Naniji, my grandmother, says flowers grow better with music, so ...." Gita's voice trailed away.

Mr. Flinch's wrinkled mouth widened into a smile. "Well, now, your Naniji is right." He scratched his chin. "Seeing as how you made this, er, suppose you come over and help me hang it?"

Slowly, Gita stood up. She waved through the kitchen window to Mummy, who nodded her head.

Gita eased through the shrubby corner and followed the winding path to the rose arbour.

"Now then," said Mr. Flinch, "where shall we hang this?"

Gita took a deep breath and stared at the flower beds filled with shades of blue, yellow, red.

"There!" She pointed to a nail sticking out from the centre of the arbour.

Mr. Flinch reached for a ladder leaning against the shed. His thin arms shook slightly.

"Let me do that," cried Gita. She clambered up the ladder and hung the wind chimes.

"Thank you," Mr. Flinch smiled. He reached up and shook her hand.

"You're welcome," said Gita, softly. The skin on the back of his hand was loose and crepey, bulging with veins — just like Naniji's.

"Now then, I've got something for you," said Mr. Flinch. He cut a bunch of roses, trimming the thorns. "You come over again, now, eh?" he said, handing Gita the bouquet.

Gita stared at him for a moment. Mr. Flinch didn't have monster eyes at all. They were soft and blue, like forget-me-nots.

"I will," Gita said. "Oh, Mr. Flinch, we're getting the First Rose for our garden today. I want one like this." Gita pointed to the rose arbour. "What kind is it?"

"It's an Explorer rose," said Mr. Flinch. "Grows great around here." He sniffed and rubbed his head. "Mind you, now, Gita, you've got to start it right — dig the hole big and wide."

"That's what Naniji says," cried Gita. "Oh, Mr. Flinch, would you come over and help me plant it?"

A sudden breeze hummed past Gita and set the wind chimes ringing. Mr. Flinch's face lit up as it had when he'd played the violin.

He cleared his throat. "Well, now, if you like, I'll do that."

Gita smiled. She'd make new wind chimes and the First Rose would dig its roots down, down towards Naniji's garden on the other side of the world. It would stretch its branches strong and high — maybe even dance over the fence to Mr. Flinch's violin.